FLESH
AND BLOOD

FLESH AND BLOOD

CHRIS PRIESTLEY

Barrington Stoke

For Torrin

First published in 2017 in Great Britain by
Barrington Stoke Ltd
18 Walker Street, Edinburgh, EH3 7LP

www.barringtonstoke.co.uk

Text & Illustrations © 2017 Chris Priestley

The moral right of Chris Priestley to be identified as the author
and illustrator of this work has been asserted in accordance
with the Copyright, Designs and Patents Act, 1988

A CIP catalogue record for this book is available
from the British Library upon request

ISBN: 978-1-78112-688-2

Printed in China by Leo

Contents

Chapter 1

The Dead House

Bill had made it plain he didn't want to talk to his sister, but Jane followed him out into the back yard and carried on anyway.

"It's all right for you," she said. "They weren't mean to you!"

Bill found it hard to look at her. "They weren't mean to you either, you little liar," he said.

"Don't call me a liar!" she yelled, and her face was fierce with rage.

"Don't lie then," Bill replied with a snarl.

"I'm not lying," Jane said. "They weren't mean when you were around. They were mean in secret."

"Ha!" Bill said, and he turned to face her. "You were homesick, that's all. Silly baby. Now look. We could be in the country right now. Playing in the woods, in the fields, down by the river. But oh no, because of you we've had to come back to London and now we'll get blown to pieces."

"Stop saying that!" Jane said, and her eyes were wet with tears. "No we won't. Mummy says we'll be safe as long as we do everything we're supposed to do and –"

"People get blown to pieces every night, Jane," Bill said. He poked the drain in the yard with a stick. "Every night. We're no different. It could happen tonight."

"I hate you!" Jane said.

"I hate you too!" Bill said with a shrug.

Jane kicked the air between them and stomped back into the house. Bill could hear her telling their mother her side of the argument.

Bill's mother stormed out into the yard. "You apologise this instant, Bill Marshall," she said.

"Why should I?" Bill said. "Why is it always –"

"I'm not going to argue with you, Bill," his mother said. "You say sorry or you go to bed with no supper."

Bill glared at his sister.

"Sorry," he mumbled.

His mother knew that this was the most she could expect. "That's better," she said. "What would your father say? He could walk in the front door any day and he won't want to hear all this nonsense now, will he? After all he's suffered?"

Bill shrugged. He hadn't seen his father for the best part of a year. He wasn't sure he even remembered what he looked like – not really. When he thought of his father it was the dog-eared photograph by his bed that he saw in his mind, not the real-life man. Bill wondered what he looked like now.

Bill's father had been captured by the Germans and he was in a prisoner-of-war camp. He'd been the gunner in a bomber that had been shot down over Belgium in September – six months before. He had been in the P.O.W. camp ever since.

A lot of kids in the streets where Bill lived had been evacuated to the country in September 1939, right at the start of the war. Everyone was so sure that bombs were going to rain down as soon as war was declared. But it never happened. By Christmas a third of the kids had come back.

Bill and Jane hadn't been sent away in that first wave. Their mother couldn't bear the family to be apart. But after the fall of Dunkirk in May 1940, she packed Bill and Jane off to their aunts in Suffolk.

A lot of children went on their own, sobbing, with their names on tags, loaded onto railway carriages like parcels. The billeting officers farmed them out to anyone who would have them. At least Bill and Jane were staying with family. Their mother had taken them there.

Bill had never left London in his life and it felt like he was running away. He didn't care about bombs – or he told himself he didn't. He felt like his place was in London – at home in the big, bustling city he knew so well. He might as well have been going to the moon.

Bill would never have admitted it, but he wasn't as brave as he pretended. He'd been more scared of the countryside than he was of the German planes.

He knew every drain cover and kerbstone of the streets at home and the thought of fields and dark woods made him feel dizzy. It wasn't natural to have that much green. It wasn't right. All that open space. London was filthy and black with soot, but Bill didn't care. He knew it. It was his. He felt safe there.

Jane had sobbed and sobbed on their first night and he'd been happy to comfort her – it helped to stop him from crying, like he'd wanted to.

At first, Bill's fears about the countryside seemed to have been proved right. The local children spoke in a strange, slow accent and then they had the cheek to make fun of the way Bill and Jane spoke. Bill had two fights with local boys in as many days. He and Jane kept to themselves after that.

But then something clicked. Bill woke up one day and looked out at the sun rising between the trees. He heard the birds singing and it was like a huge weight had been lifted from his back. All the effort he had put into refusing to take any pleasure in this new place fell away. Instead of fighting with the local boys, he worked at getting to know them. At last he started to enjoy it.

And he never stopped enjoying it. Right up until their aunts told them that they were to go back to London. The aunts didn't say, but Bill knew that Jane's endless letters of complaint had got their result. The bombs had never come, so their mother thought that London was safe again. Bill knew he should have been glad, but he wasn't.

But no sooner had they come home than their father was shot down and all hell broke loose over London. The bombs that hadn't fallen the year before, now came down in their hundreds. There was death and destruction everywhere. But there was no more talk of sending Bill and Jane away. And now here they were, fighting in the back yard.

Bill and Jane had always fought, as brothers and sisters will, but the feeling between them was different now. Jane knew how much Bill had loved it in the country and how happy he was there. Bill wondered if that was why she'd complained. He would never forgive her. Never.

He felt ashamed and angry at himself and at Jane, and at the whole world for making him feel that way. He kicked out at the wall, harder than he'd intended and he howled as his toe struck the brick.

Bill limped out of the back yard and down the alley to the street. Some boys he knew were playing at the far end, but he wasn't in the mood. They'd been happy enough to have him back, but he felt changed and they all seemed different – because they were the same as when he'd left them.

Bill found himself standing outside the Dead House at the end of his street. It was bigger than the rest, with a brick gable end with a billboard space on it. The poster there at the moment was a Dig For Victory one. Its bright reds and yellows were the only flash of colour in the street and they seemed all the more odd stuck on the side of this creepy house with its blank, boarded-up windows and door.

The house had been empty for as long as Bill could remember and even his mother couldn't remember the last time anyone lived there. It had been deserted since well before the war even started.

The local children had put the glass out of the windows years ago and they looked as dull and lifeless as the eye-sockets in a skull. Children whispered stories in playgrounds and on street corners of the many ghosts who haunted it and of the murders committed there. Bill never believed a word of them, but he still couldn't linger there alone. He turned his back on the house, and had to stop himself from running away.

Chapter 2
The Wish

The sirens sounded for an air raid and Bill made for the public shelter under the railway arches with his family and neighbours. Searchlight beams criss-crossed the night sky, and lit up a barrage balloon floating above them.

Soon there would be the hum of the bombers, the blast of the anti-aircraft guns, the thud of the bombs, and the lottery of where the bombs would land. They seemed to get closer every night.

There was no panic. It seemed like people could get used to anything, and the air raids had become part of their routine, an irritation. People were resigned. If a bomb had your name on it, then that was that – there was nothing you could do about it.

But that didn't mean people weren't scared or didn't hate the shelters. Everyone hated the shelters. But it was a point of pride to look like none of it bothered you. Bill understood this, and he tried not to show how much he hated it all – how much he wanted to hear birdsong instead of the whine of bombs.

He could hear Jane whimpering in the dark of the shelter as the *CLUMP* of the bombs came closer. Her fear annoyed him even more than her refusal to believe they were in danger. It reminded him that they could be miles and miles away from here if it wasn't for her.

Bill thought how it would all be so different if he had a brother. A brother would never have wanted to leave those woods and fields and barns. A brother would have understood. Bill was sure of it.

He'd always felt this was at the core of why he and Jane didn't get on. He didn't know any brothers and sisters who saw eye to eye. Jane felt it too. She'd even begged for a sister until their mother made it clear that – with their father in a German P.O.W. camp – it was unlikely. "Besides," Mum had said, "you two are all the family I've ever wanted."

So that meant that Bill wasn't going to get a brother either. He would have liked a younger brother to look after and stick up for. He imagined taking his little brother to the country and smiled at the thought of the fun they'd have.

It wasn't like he didn't love his mother or want to be with her. He did. But he might never get another chance like that for the rest of his entire life. Jane had taken it from him.

The streets that had seemed like home before he left now seemed alien. The war had changed everything. The friends he'd missed so much now seemed dull and coarse. They seemed like they had been made by the war too. The children in the village in the country had seemed unmarked by it.

A muffled thump above the shelter made everyone jump and a baby started to cry. An old woman from down the street started to pray to herself and another woman sang 'My Old Man Said Follow the Van'. One by one others joined in and, as they sang, Bill found himself mouthing his own silent words. Not a prayer exactly ...

"I wish I had a brother instead of a sister," Bill whispered to himself, his voice drowned out by the singing. He stared at the dim shape of Jane who was cuddled against their mother.

"I wish I had a brother instead of a sister." Bill knew he couldn't be seen or heard. He whispered the words with more seriousness than he had said anything ever before in his life.

"I wish I had a brother instead of a sister."

He said these words three times, because three times seemed right for a wish. And that's what it was, Bill realised. A wish spoken three times. Just like in a fairy tale.

A brother was what he wished for more than anything. More – he realised with a cold shudder of guilt – than he wished for the return of his father, more than he wished to be back in Suffolk. Because what would be the point of that, if he had to go with Jane?

All of a sudden there was a much louder thump. It sounded like a crane had dropped something heavy from the sky. The ground shook and dust fell on them.

The song stopped and people cried out. Jane shrieked. Their mother grabbed them both and pulled them close. Bill let her. He was scared. He could feel his body tense as they waited for the next *CLUMP*. The one that might smash straight into the shelter.

Their mother whispered how much she loved them and how they were all going to be all right, she was sure of it. She didn't sound sure at all.

Bill wondered if he was about to be punished – punished for telling Jane they might get blown to pieces, for wishing for a brother, for not wishing his father home, for not believing his mother when she said they would be safe.

Maybe another bomb was falling through the cold night air, plummeting down, down, down towards their shelter. Maybe this thought would be his last. Bill closed his eyes. He flinched.

But there was no new blast, no more bombs. The planes moved on. As the whole shelter held its breath, the next sound they heard was the all-clear and then a great cheer went up and Bill joined in.

Their mother pulled them even closer like she always did at the all-clear.

"There now," she said, and her voice wobbled as she spoke. "Didn't I say that everything would be fine?"

Chapter 3

The Rescue

As they left the shelter, they saw a plume of smoke over the roof of the pub. That must be the bomb they'd heard. The one that had sounded so close as it landed.

Bill wondered if their house had been destroyed. He wondered this with a much happier heart than he should have. If it had been, maybe they would have to move.

If they had to move, then maybe they could all move out of London – to the country to stay with his aunts again. If his mother was there too, Jane would be fine. And then, when his father came back, they'd all be together. Maybe they could find a house and live there.

But Bill's little fantasy soon came to an end because it became clear it wasn't their house that had been hit. It was the Dead House. It had a massive hole in one end and smoke was pouring out next to the Dig For Victory poster. When they walked round to stand with the crowd they could see flames and smoke billowing from downstairs and even more from between the roof tiles.

There was both shock and relief in Bill's mother's face that a bomb had come this close to the family home but it had escaped. They hurried past the people helping to clear the rubble.

"No one's lived there for years," a woman said to an ARP warden who was standing near by.

"Even so, Missus," the warden said. "We have to check. You never know. There might be someone taking shelter there or sleeping rough."

"I think we'd know if someone was sleeping rough," another woman said.

But the warden wasn't listening. Instead he was heading off to stop a huddle of children getting too close.

"They think they're something special when they put that bloomin' helmet on," the first woman said with a nod at the warden's back. The second woman chuckled.

Bill stood and stared at the activity around him. This was the closest the Blitz had come to them and it was scary, but it was also exciting.

Tomorrow he would search for bomb fragments to add to his collection.

"You've all had a lucky escape," the warden said when he came back. "Nice of Jerry to hit an empty house."

"Yes," Bill's mother said. "But a bit close for comfort."

"They got my mother's place last week," the warden said. "She was down the shelter, but even so. She'll never be the same, bless her."

Bill's mother and the warden went on talking, but Bill had begun to tune them out. He tuned everything out, until a strange calm came over him. It was totally at odds with the frantic activity around him.

What was even stranger was that Bill was not in control of this feeling of calm. The sound of the world faded so far that he shook his head. Was he was going deaf? But then ...

In the midst of this odd calm he heard a voice. It was there and then gone so fast that Bill couldn't tell whether he had heard or thought it. The sound of it was like a thought – like his own brain talking.

Bill strained his ears. There it was again!

A boy's voice coming from the house, the burning Dead House.

"Help me. Help me."

"Stop!" Bill shouted. "There's someone in there!"

The crowd of helpers all turned to face him and then to where he was pointing – at the hole where a window had once been. It was gaping black, and belching smoke and flames.

"I can't hear anything," the warden said.

"Bill?" his mother said. "Are you sure?"

"Yes!" said Bill. "There it goes again. There's someone trapped."

"Can we trust him, Missus?" a large man asked.

"Yes," Bill's mother said. "He's never been one for making things up."

"That's good enough for me."

With that, the big man strode off. He put his coat over his head to shield against the smoke, then he went inside with no regard for the fire blazing through the house.

Chapter 4

The Ambulance

Bill and Jane and their mother stood across the street and waited.

After what seemed like an age there was a gasp from the crowd and the man came out with a blackened bundle in his arms. He staggered towards them, coughing violently.

The man laid the bundle carefully on the ground before collapsing into a fit of more racking coughs. Bill stared at the bundle of burnt rags and realised it was a child – a boy of about his own age.

"Is he alive?" Bill asked.

The man nodded, still coughing.

"Just about. But not for much longer if he don't get no proper help."

Bill started towards the boy, but the man grabbed his arm.

"He's in a bad way, Missus," he said to Bill's mother. He croaked and spluttered out the warning. "Don't let him see. Don't look yourself neither."

Bill's mother went pale and pulled Bill back. Bill stared at the smoke rising up from the boy before his mother put her hand on his face and pushed it round so he couldn't see.

"Oh the poor thing," his mother said. "He needs to get to hospital and soon."

"He's a goner if you ask me," said the woman who worked in the baker's shop.

"Shhh!" Bill's mother said. "Don't. That's a horrible thing to say."

"All I'm saying is, if you ask me –"

"Well, no one is asking you, Nora," a woman behind them said and the crowd laughed.

"If he can just get to hospital ..." Bill's mother said.

As if on cue, an ambulance came racing towards them with its bells ringing. The wheels skidded to a halt in the debris strewn across the road.

"What have we got here?" an ambulance woman said as she ran over.

"A boy's been brought out of that building," the warden said. "This here lad heard him calling. That chap over there went in and saved him. Deserves a ruddy medal he does."

The man waved this praise away and coughed some more. The ambulance woman laid the boy on a stretcher.

"Any more?" she asked.

The man who had saved the boy shook his head. "If there are, they're done for I reckon," he said. "But I didn't – *cough* – see no one else. The boy was just sitting in the middle of the floor, like he was waiting for someone, with flames all around him. Strangest – *cough* – thing I've ever seen. But I reckon he was on his own."

"Jolly good. You should come too, sir," the ambulance woman said.

"I'm all right," he said, wheezing again.

"Don't be silly," she said. "Get in."

The man shrugged and did as he was told. The ambulance started up again, swung round and headed off into the night, just as fast as it had come.

The crowd stood for a while and watched the firemen at work before the warden got them all to move away.

"Go home now," he said. "There's nothing to be done here. Get them kids home."

"What about the boy?" Bill asked. "What'll happen to him?"

"I don't know," the warden said. "He's in good hands now. He owes you a thank you, don't he? I don't know how you managed to hear him above all that racket, but I reckon he'd be a goner if you hadn't."

"I wonder who he is," Bill's mother added.

"Who knows?" the warden said. "That's one for the police I reckon."

Chapter 5

The Policeman

Bill couldn't sleep that night. Every time his eyes closed, he heard the boy's voice and saw his smoking form lying in the rubble on the ground.

It was less like a memory and more like it was happening right there and then – like it was happening all over again. Bill felt he was there. He felt the same strange sense of danger, the same excitement.

When at last Bill slept, his sleep was filled with vivid dreams – of the boy, his cries from the Dead House, his smoking body. If anything, it felt even more real. Again and again, Bill heard that voice, saw the bundle in the man's arms. He could smell the smoke, feel the heat from the flames.

At breakfast, Jane was full of questions. Bill wanted to talk about the boy too, but not with Jane.

As they cleared the table, there was a loud knock at the front door and they all jumped. Bill went to open it. It was a tall man dressed in a suit and coat and hat, dark against the morning light.

Bill stared in confusion for a moment. Could this be his father back from the war? He looked older. Could he have changed that much? This dream-like dizzy wonder only lasted a few long seconds. He could see now that it was someone else. A stranger.

"Morning, son," the man said. "Police. Detective Sergeant Henson. Is your mother about?"

"Mum!" Bill shouted. "There's a copper here!"

"Bill!" his mother said. "Honestly. Apologies for my son. I blame the films he watches at the Saturday pictures."

The policeman smiled and took off his hat.

"I've been called worse, Ma'am," he said.

"What can we do for you ...?"

"Detective Sergeant Henson, Ma'am. We're following up enquiries about that boy that was found last night."

"Oh," Bill's mother said. "Have you found his parents? Do you know who he is?"

"I'm afraid not, Ma'am," D.S. Henson said. He took out a notebook and opened it. "Could I perhaps ask you one or two questions? It won't take long."

"Of course," Bill's mother said. "If it will help. Won't you come in, Detective Sergeant? I've not long made a pot of tea. Would you like a cuppa?"

D.S. Henson followed Bill and his mother to the kitchen and they sat down at the table.

"Jane? Bill?" their mother said. "Why don't you run along and play?"

"I'd rather the young man stayed, if that's all right," D.S. Henson said.

"I suppose so," she said. "If you think it's important. But off you go and play, Jane."

Jane scowled at Bill before she shuffled away to her room.

"You're Mrs Marshall, is that right?" Henson said.

"That's right."

"Is there a Mr Marshall, might I ask?"

"There is," Bill's mother said. "He's a guest of Mr Hitler's just now."

"Ma'am?" Henson said with a puzzled frown.

"A prisoner of war. His plane got shot down and ..."

"Sorry to hear that, Ma'am," he said. "Still – he'll be home safe and sound soon I'm sure."

"Thank you. We hope so."

"He may be safer where he is than here, the way things are going," Henson said. "And this young man is ...?"

"Bill," Bill said. "Bill Marshall."

Henson wrote in his notebook. Bill frowned. There was something about the way he noted his name that he didn't like.

"I'm told it was you who heard the boy and alerted the warden," Henson said.

Bill nodded.

Henson tapped the end of his pencil against his lips as he thought about the next question, then he turned to Bill's mother.

"How about you, Ma'am?" he asked.

"Yes?" she said, confused by his meaning.

"Did you hear the boy?" he asked. He took a sip of tea.

"No I didn't," Bill's mother said. "But thank goodness Bill did."

"Indeed. Only I've asked everyone I can find who was there last night and not one person recalls hearing a thing. Even those people who were standing right next to the house. You and your son were both some way off. Don't you think that's odd?"

Bill looked at his mother and saw her frown.

"I'm not sure I know what you mean," she said. "Bill must have heard something, mustn't he? The boy was there."

D.S. Henson nodded and looked down at his notebook. Then he turned to Bill.

"Is that how it happened, Bill?" he said.

"Of course it's how it happened," Bill's mother said, and her voice was fierce. "I hope you're not going to sit in my kitchen, drinking my tea and calling my son a liar. Otherwise you and I are going to fall out."

"I'm just doing my job, Ma'am," the policeman said with a small smile. "I appreciate you helping me make sense of it all. I'm sure if that boy in the hospital was your son you'd want me to do the same."

Bill saw the colour rise in his mother's face.

"Of course," she said. "But Bill's already said what happened."

"Even so. Do you know that house, Bill?" D.S. Henson said.

Bill looked at his mother and wondered whether to answer. She nodded.

"A bit," Bill said. "I've never been in there. No one's ever had the nerve."

"Why's that?"

"People say it's haunted," Bill said.

Henson grinned at this.

"So I've heard. Do you think it's haunted?"

Bill shrugged.

"You don't think anyone might have gone in there for a dare?" he persisted.

"No one I know," Bill said.

"You're sure?" D.S. Henson said.

"Why are you asking Bill these questions?" Bill's mother asked. "It can't be a crime to think a house is haunted. Not even in wartime."

"I'm more interested in the idea that youngsters may dare each other to go in."

"Bill's said he doesn't know anyone who did that," Bill's mother snapped. "Is it so important?"

"Well," Henson said after a pause. "That would explain Bill hearing a voice that no one else could hear, wouldn't it? If he knew the boy was there. Not a lie, so much as a secret ..."

Bill's mother turned to look at her son. Bill could see that this idea made sense to her. He knew she found it strange that she'd heard nothing.

"Bill?" she said.

"I swear," Bill said. "I never saw that boy in my life before. I never knew he was in that house. Ask any of the others and you'll hear the same. I ain't hardly played with any of those kids since I got back."

"Got back?" Henson said.

"He and his sister were evacuated," Bill's mother said. "We brought them back because we thought it was safe."

"Ah," Henson said.

"And because Jane whined," Bill added.

"Shhh, Bill," his mother said. "Whatever's got into you?"

"Well, if you say you heard the boy, that's good enough for me, Bill," Henson said, and he got to his feet. "I've taken up enough of your time."

"Is it possible for you to let us know about the boy?" Bill's mother said. "If you're passing, that is."

"Of course," Henson said. "You're on my way home from the station. If we hear anything I'll let you know."

"What about the boy himself?" Bill's mother asked as they walked down the hall. "Hasn't he been able to tell you anything?"

D.S. Henson looked at Bill.

"That's another strange thing," he said, and he pushed his hand back through his hair. "He can't – or won't – talk. He hasn't said a word since they took him in. If it wasn't that Bill heard him, we wouldn't know he could talk at all."

They both looked at Bill.

"It's like something from a mystery film, isn't it?" Bill's mother said.

"It is indeed, Ma'am," the policeman said. "A miracle my mum would say. But then she's a proper Catholic."

"But not you?" Bill's mother said.

"I don't know what I believe any more," he said. He put his hat back on, and tipped the brim. "Good day, Mrs Marshall. Bill. If anything else comes to you, do let me know. However small it might seem."

Bill and his mother watched him stride down the street.

"Cheek of the man," Bill's mother said when he'd turned the corner. "Making out you weren't telling the truth."

"He was just doing his job," Bill said. "Like he said."

She smiled as she put her apron back on and fumbled to tie the straps. She smoothed the apron out and then looked at Bill.

"You don't know anything about that boy, do you?"

"No – course not," Bill told her. "I thought you were cross with that copper for accusing me. Don't you believe me?"

"Of course I do," she said, and she kissed the top of Bill's head. "And you know I don't like you saying copper. It makes you sound common."

"Mum," Bill said as they closed the door and walked back to the kitchen. "Can we visit him? The boy that they found in the house. If no one knows who he is, he can't have any visitors, can he? I feel bad for him. I can feel bad for him, can't I – even if I don't know him?"

His mother turned to look at him.

"That's very thoughtful, Bill," she said. "See what a nice young man you are."

"But can we?" Bill asked. He sensed she was flattering him before fobbing him off.

His mother put her cup of tea down – it had gone cold – and looked at him.

"We don't know where he is now, do we?" she said.

"We could find out. It can't be too hard. I bet it even says it in the paper."

His mother smiled.

"The thing is, love," she said. "You saw what a state he was in. He might not ... We don't know how he is at all, do we?"

"Well, that's why we should find out," said Bill.

"You saw how bad he was, Bill," she went on, and her face was serious. "Them were bad burns he had. How do you feel about visiting him if he's all, you know, marked and such like. You have to think about that. It's not fair to him now, is it – if you burst into tears as soon as you see him?"

"I won't burst into tears," Bill said.

"But how do you know, Bill?" she said. "No one knows how they'll react to something, do they? Until it happens."

She was right. Bill had no idea how he would feel if he saw something terrible. He just knew he had to find the boy. He had to.

Chapter 6

At the Police Station

D.S. Henson opened the door and invited
them in. Bill had never been inside a police
station before. He was expecting it to be more
exciting – it wasn't like in the films at all. Still,
Bill was glad to be here, and glad they had left
Jane with a friend. It was an adventure and he
was happy to have it without her.

They followed Henson to a small, drab
office. He ushered them in and asked them to

sit. He sat down at the other side of his desk and took out his notebook and pen.

"I should say straight away that we don't have any new information," Bill's mother said.

A look of disappointment crossed the policeman's face. He put his pen down and sat back in his seat with his hands clasped.

"I'm sorry," Bill's mother said. "I hope we aren't wasting your time."

"Not at all, Ma'am," he said. "But I'm wondering why you've come to see me."

"Well, Bill and me, we were hoping you might have some information for us."

"Oh?" Henson said, and he looked from one face to the other. "That's a new one. What can I help you with?"

"It's about the boy," Bill said. "You know, the boy from the house. Only, what with me finding him and everything ... You know – I'm interested in him."

"Which is only natural, I suppose," Henson said.

There was something about Henson's tone that made Bill think he still didn't quite believe Bill's version of events. But then, he thought, maybe policemen always sound suspicious. Maybe a suspicious voice was an important part of the job.

"Do you have any idea who he might be yet?" Bill's mother asked.

"None at all, I'm afraid, Ma'am," Henson replied. "There's no record of anyone at that address and no one has been reported missing – or no one who fits this boy's description."

"But how can that happen?" Bill's mother asked. "How can a boy just disappear and no one claim him? He must belong to someone."

"You'd be surprised, Ma'am," Henson said. "When this whole terrible war is over, there are going to be a lot of broken families and missing children. Maybe the boy's parents were killed in an air raid and he's been sleeping rough. Maybe he doesn't remember who he is. I've seen that, Ma'am. Saw it in the last war – people see things that are too much for them and it sends them over the edge."

"How awful," Bill's mother said. "Poor boy."

Henson seemed lost in his own thoughts for a moment. He looked up after a few seconds, and blinked as if he was looking into a bright light.

"The thing is, we just don't know," he said. "We don't know who he is or where he's from. We've tried to talk to him but he's not talking – if he can talk at all. He may have been hurt in the blast or he may not have been able to talk in the first place. Or maybe he doesn't want to say anything just now and he'll talk when he's good and ready. Can't be easy for him in that hospital on his own."

"No," Bill's mother agreed.

"That's why we're here, really," Bill said. "We want to visit him. Would that be all right?"

The policeman smiled at Bill's question.

"I don't see why not," he said. "He's in a special ward because of his burns. I can tell the hospital to expect visitors. Normally it would be family only in a case as serious as this, but if I explain who you are, I'm sure they'll bend the rules."

"Would you?" Bill's mother said. "That's very kind."

"I'm a very kind man," said Henson, and he smiled some more. "Leave it with me and I'll see what I can do."

Chapter 7

The Hospital

As it turned out, Henson was as good as his word. The very next day, he knocked at the door and asked if they wanted to visit the boy.

"I've got the car outside," he said. "I can take you there right now, if you like."

"Are you sure we're important enough to use your petrol rations on?" Bill's mother asked with a smile.

"You are important witnesses to an open case," Henson said.

"We're important witnesses, Bill," his mother said. "Imagine that!"

Bill, his mother and Jane put their coats on. Jane wasn't going to miss out on a ride in a car. There was a woman driver in the front, who jumped out and opened the door for Bill's mother. She and Bill and Jane got in the back. Sergeant Henson got in the front and the driver started the car. Henson turned to them and smiled as they set off.

Bill's face was pressed to the window every minute of the drive, even more so when they crossed the river and the view opened up. It was a shock to see how much damage the bombs had done. Bill wondered how much more it would take to reduce the whole city to rubble.

When they reached the hospital the driver opened the door for them again. Henson told her to wait and she drove off to park.

The staff at the front desk directed Henson to the ward. They followed as a nurse clip-clopped along a maze of polished corridors to Ward 6B. Henson introduced himself to the matron who nodded at everything he had to say before whispering a few words Bill couldn't hear. A nurse opened the door behind them and they heard a distant scream.

"I think it might be an idea for Jane to wait with me," Henson said. "You'll keep me company, won't you, Jane?"

Jane nodded, and there was a look of relief on her face. She went over to pick a book from the table next to the door. Bill and his mother walked on with the matron.

"I can't let you stay for long," the matron said, with a flare of her nostrils. "The poor little chap is in shock and in a lot of pain. But we've not heard so much as a squeak from him. He may be too exhausted. Pain is very tiring, you know."

"Of course," Bill's mother said. "We only want to say hello. It must be awful to have no visitors."

The matron didn't reply, but her mouth grew even more pinched. Bill had the distinct impression that she would be happier if there were no visitors at all to mess up her lovely clean hospital. Bill's mother turned to Bill and made a face like the matron's sour look. Bill had to stop himself from giggling.

But Bill's mood changed as they walked into the ward and he saw the beds filled with wounded people. The room was gloomy on this dull day, and the windows were criss-crossed with tape to stop them bursting into the room in a bomb blast. There were strange smells and sounds, and none of them were good.

Bill tried to look straight ahead. He stared at the buttons on the back of his mother's coat, and tried to ignore the moans and whimpers and sobbing and the comforting words of nurses.

Bill knew that London must be full of the dead and injured of the Blitz, but he'd never given them much thought before. There must be ward after ward like this all over the city – he knew that. But, Bill asked himself, what was to stop them from being bombed here in their hospital beds? No one could stop that happening too.

What a thing to say you'd done – hurled bombs down on ordinary people far below and then flown home for a cup of tea like it was nothing. If the German pilots drank tea, that was. Any one of those bombs might kill a hundred people. You could kill thousands in a night. How did those pilots live with themselves? Bill knew that this was what his father's plane was doing when it was shot down – bombing towns and cities below. It was the war, but even so ...

They came to another door and some side wards with just one bed in them. The matron held the door open and they walked in. It was so quiet once the door was closed again. 'It's like being in a chapel,' Bill thought. Almost silent but for the faint noise of the street outside.

The boy was lying face up with his head on the pillow and his arms on top of the blanket. A drip was feeding into his hand. His head was covered in bandage – all apart from two holes. One was for his right eye, and the other for his mouth. Both eye and mouth were open as he turned to face them.

"Hello ..." Bill's mother said in a low voice. "I hope we aren't disturbing you. Don't be scared. You don't know us ... But we were there the night they found you. It was Bill here who heard you call out."

The boy turned his head and looked at Bill.

"Yeah," Bill said. He felt he had to say something. "I told them I could hear someone and then this big bloke, he went in and grabbed you. Do you remember?"

The boy moved his head from side to side – *no.*

"I'm not surprised," Bill said. "You were in a pretty bad way. We weren't sure if –"

Bill's mother gave him a nudge and frowned at him.

"What?" He frowned back. "*What?*"

"Are they treating you well?" Bill's mother said.

The boy nodded this time.

"We asked the police if we could come and see you. They're trying to find your family. Do you remember why you were in that house?"

The boy shook his head for *no* and closed his eye.

"The police have asked you all this already, haven't they?" Bill's mother said.

A nod so small you could miss it. *Yes.*

"Sorry," she said. "We won't ask you any more questions. We wanted to say hello and let you know we're thinking of you. It was Bill's idea actually."

The boy did not move.

"We've been told not to tire you, so ..."

The matron took them back to where Jane and D.S. Henson were waiting.

"How did it go?" he asked.

"That poor boy," Bill's mother said.

"He's still not talking?"

She shook her head.

"But he can hear all right," Bill said.

"Yes," his mother said. "Bill's right. He responded when we asked him questions."

"It's been a terrible ordeal for him," Henson said. "Maybe he'll talk when he's ready."

"I feel so sorry for him stuck in here," Bill's mother said. "That matron isn't the friendliest of women, is she?"

Henson raised his eyebrows.

"I should say," he replied. "She just came in and told me and Jane off for talking too much. She made me jump. No one's made me jump since my dad used to tell me off when I was Bill's age."

When they went out to the car, the gloom of the day had turned to rain.

As Henson's driver took them back home, Bill was too lost in his own thoughts about the boy in the hospital to notice the passing view this time, apart from a glimpse of St Paul's Cathedral against the grey sky.

Chapter 8

Bill's Idea

Bill and his mother went back to see the boy as often as they could. It wasn't easy. Sometimes they made their own way, sometimes Henson and his driver took them.

The visits followed the same pattern as the first. Jane would wait outside, the stern matron would insist they didn't stay long, the boy would listen but wouldn't speak. On the third visit, Bill had the idea to read a comic out loud and that became his habit every time.

Bill and his mother persisted, even though there was little sign from the boy that they meant anything to him. They couldn't even tell themselves that their visits cheered him up – but now they had started they both felt it would be cruel and wrong to stop. Bill felt a keen sense of responsibility for the boy, though he couldn't have explained why.

When D.S. Henson brought them, he would sometimes – with much frowning from the matron – join them in the boy's room. He hoped, no doubt, to get some clue as to his identity. But he was always disappointed. The boy never spoke.

When they came home after one visit, Bill and his mother stood next to Henson's car in their street. The rain had eased off but the pavement was wet and shining. The policeman shook them by the hand and tipped his hat.

"Goodbye, Henson," Bill's mother said. "Thanks again for taking us. It's good of you to spare the time for us – and the boy."

"I'm sure he appreciates your visits," Henson said.

"But a boy needs his mum at that age," Bill's mother said. She put her arm round Bill. "They think they don't, but they do. Poor little so-and-so."

"Well, yes. I'd better be –"

Bill pulled free of his mother's grip all of a sudden. "He could come and live with us!" he said.

Bill's mother exchanged a glance with Henson.

"I'm not sure we'd be allowed to, Bill," his mother said. "He's not ours, is he? And he's very ill."

"Actually," said the policemen. "He doesn't seem to be anybody's. The doc says he's done most of what he can for now. The boy does seem to be stable – he doesn't need to be in hospital. Not that I'm trying to push you into taking him on. He's not your responsibility ..."

"Please, Mum!" Bill pleaded. He was struck by a sudden feeling that it was more important than anything that the boy came to live with them.

"Oh, Bill," his mother said. "We don't know anything about him and he's been so badly hurt."

"Of course, Ma'am," Henson said. "You've done more than most by visiting him all these weeks. Please don't think I was encouraging Bill in this."

"Not at all," Bill's mum said. "And," she gave a little laugh, "please stop calling me Ma'am. Makes me sound so old –"

"But, Mum," Bill interrupted. "If I hadn't heard him call out he'd have died, wouldn't he? I'll look after him."

"Oh, you will, will you?" his mother said. She raised her eyebrows. "You'll change his bandages for him and take him to the toilet and feed him?"

Bill shrugged.

"I can do all that," he said. "I don't mind."

Bill's mother took a deep breath.

"What if Dad was all bandaged up and no one knew who he was?" Bill said. He was determined to press home his point. "Wouldn't we want someone to take him in and look after him?"

At that, Mrs Marshall looked away down the street and Bill felt bad. He shouldn't have mentioned his father, he knew how much it upset her.

"How could we look after him?" she said at last. "We're not trained nurses. If he was just a boy with nowhere to go, then I wouldn't mind."

"The hospital would send a nurse to deal with all of that," Henson said, before adding, "Not that I'm trying to push you one way or another ..."

"How can you know?" Bill's mother said.

"It's already come up," Henson said with a sigh. "The hospital ... they were talking about where he'll live long term."

"What do you mean?" Bill's mother said. "They'll send him to a home – an orphanage?"

She closed her eyes and put her hand to her mouth.

"All right then," she said. "If the hospital and the police think he'd be better off with us, it's the least we can do."

"We'd be doing 'our bit', wouldn't we?" Bill said.

The policeman chuckled.

"I suppose we would, Bill," said his mother.

"If you're sure," Henson said. "I'll let them know. It's a very nice thing you're doing, Ma'am."

Bill's mother blushed.

"Not me – it's Bill here. He's the one who's going to take care of him."

Henson and Bill's mother laughed and Bill frowned. He suspected he was the butt of the joke, but it didn't matter. He didn't quite know why, but he was very happy at the thought of the lonely, bandaged boy becoming a part of their family.

Chapter 9

The Bandaged Boy

Bill couldn't settle on the day that the boy was to arrive. He sat by the window for hours, and rushed to the door at every hint of a noise outside.

Jane was much less excited. She was still not happy that such a major change had been agreed without her.

"What are we going to call this boy, anyway?" she said.

Bill was sitting with his face pressed up against the window. He didn't turn round.

"We have to call him something," Jane said.

In a way, she was right. The boy was known to all of them simply as 'the boy'.

But Bill wouldn't give her even that. "No we don't," he said. "We can't just give him a name. How would you like it if someone decided to call you Agnes?"

Bill had chosen this name because Jane was always falling out with a girl called Agnes who lived a few doors down.

"Not very much, I suppose," Jane agreed. "But I wouldn't like being called 'girl' either."

"It doesn't matter," Bill said. He was already bored. "He'll tell us his name when he gets his voice back."

"What if he doesn't?" she said. "What if he doesn't ever talk?"

Bill shrugged. He didn't want to talk to Jane. He knew the boy would get his voice back. He was sure of it, but he didn't want to try and explain it to her. He just wanted the boy to arrive.

Jane wandered off in one of her sulks, and it wasn't long before Bill had his wish. He'd been looking out for an ambulance, but it was a car that pulled up outside the house. D.S. Henson got out, nodded to Bill and opened the door to help the bandaged boy out.

He led the boy towards the house and Bill ran to the front door.

"Mum! Mum!" he shouted. "They're here."

Bill opened the door and there was Henson with his hat in his hand, and the boy standing in front of him. The boy was about Bill's height, which meant that Bill had a rather startling view of his bandaged face. It was still bandaged just like in hospital, with only his right eye and his mouth free. Bill tried not to stare, but he couldn't help himself. The boy's one uncovered eye stared right back.

"Don't just stand there, Bill," his mother said. "Let them in."

Bill snapped out of his dream and stepped to one side. He pressed himself back into the wall and Henson and the boy walked in. The boy turned his head to look at Bill as he went past.

Jane hid behind their mother, clinging to her skirt and peeping out with a worried frown. Bill realised that she had never seen the boy before. Bill's mother leaned forward with a smile, as though the bandages weren't there.

"Welcome to our home," she said to the boy. "We're very happy to have you here. Aren't we, children?"

Bill agreed right away, but Jane just made a noise like a whimper.

"Well then," Henson said. "The nurse will be along later to talk a few things over with you. She – or another nurse – will be here every day, so you shouldn't have anything to worry about."

"We'll be fine, won't we, Bill?" Bill's mother said.

"Yes, sir," said Bill.

"Will you stay for a cup of tea?" Bill's mother said. "The kettle's on."

"I'm afraid I can't," Henson said. "We're rushed off our feet at the moment."

"What a shame," she said. "You will pop in and see how we're all getting along, won't you?"

"You try and stop me," Henson said with a wave goodbye.

And then he was gone and the door closed, and they were alone with their new member of the household. Bill was struck by how the house seemed to have shrunk a couple of sizes.

"Come and sit down," Bill's mother said. "You must be tired."

The boy nodded and followed them into the sitting room. Bill's mother showed him to the sofa and helped him to sit.

They all stood looking at him and then felt bad for staring, so Bill's mother said, "Bill, why don't you show your guest where he'll be sleeping?"

Bill smiled and nodded and looked at the boy, who got to his feet and followed Bill up the stairs. Bill's mother and Jane watched after them as the boy climbed the stairs, slowly and painfully. Bill stood at the top and held out his hand.

The boy was to sleep in Bill's bed and Bill was to sleep on a fold-out bed his mother had borrowed. Bill had tried it out and found that it creaked like a rusty gate and was almost as uncomfortable as the floor. But he didn't mind. It was the least he could do.

The boy didn't react to anything Bill said about the bed or the room or the clothes that they'd found for him – old clothes of Bill's. As he listened to what Bill said, he looked at him straight in the face with his uncovered eye the whole time. When Bill had finished, the boy turned and walked back downstairs, where he took his place on the sofa again.

Bill had become used to the boy's silence during their many hospital visits and yet he was disappointed. It wasn't so much the silence as the utter lack of interest. Bill told himself that it wasn't that he expected gratitude, it was just that he'd imagined the boy would show some response at being in their house.

Bill pulled out his old toy box and dug around until he found some lead soldiers of his father's. He held them up to the boy's face, then put them in the boy's hands, but he still refused to play. After a while, Bill gave up and sat next to the boy on the sofa to read a comic.

Not much later there was a knock at the door and Jane called to say the nurse had arrived. After a brief whispered chat, Bill's mother showed her into the sitting room.

"There you are!" the nurse said when she saw the boy.

The boy looked at her.

"The ward isn't the same without you," the nurse said.

The boy turned away from her and looked instead at Bill.

"I just have to have a little look at his bandages," the nurse said, and Bill saw her make a funny face and nod at him.

"Bill," his mother said. "Could you and Jane leave so the nurse can get on?"

"I won't get in the way," Bill said.

"Even so," his mother said. "Off you go."

Jane was happy to head off to her room, but Bill hung around at the bottom of the stairs and listened to the conversation on the other side of the door, which was still ajar.

"You might want to pop out yourself, Ma'am," the nurse said. "I'm fine here on my own. We're old friends."

Bill saw the boy's hands clench into fists as the nurse reached towards his face. His mother left the room and closed the door behind her.

"Come on," she said with a weak smile. "Let's have a cup of tea, shall we."

They were onto their second cup when at last the nurse came out.

"Is everything all right?" Bill's mother said.

The nurse looked at Bill.

"I think Bill should hear anything you have to say," his mother said. "He's old enough."

"Very well. As you must realise, the boy's face is very bad," the nurse said. "I'm afraid it won't really get any better now. I think you need to know that."

"I see," Bill's mother said.

"They're doing some amazing work on pilots who have been horribly burned and so on," the nurse told them. "They may be able to do something in the future for this boy. One never knows."

But she didn't sound hopeful.

"I'm telling you this because when those bandages come off," she said, "it will be a hard thing to see – a hard thing to look at. Even for those of us who are used to such things."

Bill's mother nodded, and looked back towards the sitting room.

The nurse's face was pale and her voice soft as she went on. "It's very kind of you, to take him in, but you must ask yourself – will you be able to deal with how the boy will look without his bandages?"

Chapter 10

Silence

Bill tried to imagine the most awful face beneath the boy's bandages, but he knew that it would be far worse than anything he could think of.

But Bill wanted to be brave.

He was desperate to prove that he could cope with whatever lay below the bandages. Jane might scream or cry, but Bill would greet that ruined face as if he had seen it every day of his life.

Bill had often wondered if his father might come home damaged and he'd always hoped he would be able to deal with it if it happened. His dad would always be his dad whatever he looked like. The same was true of this boy. He was a boy just like Bill, no matter what had happened to his face.

Bill knew the most important thing was to behave as normally as possible and give the boy no reason to suspect any fear or horror Bill might have about his face.

But this was hard. There were no two ways about it – the boy made him nervous. He didn't speak – or make any noise at all – and he seemed to be able to sit or stand in one position for long periods of time. He didn't move any part of his body save for the odd shift

of his head as he watched Bill or Jane or their
mother.

The boy seemed fascinated with Jane and
would stand and watch as she played. She
would try her very hardest to talk to him and
include him in her game, all without actually
looking at him. Then, when this failed, she
would try to ignore him. But in the end she
would whimper and move away to some other
place in the house to get away from him.

Bill was very happy that the boy shared a
room with him, but even so he found it just as
hard as Jane to talk to someone who never ever
talked back. More and more, Bill felt like the
boy was staying silent from choice – that he
could speak if he wanted to.

And, just as Bill felt sorry for the boy, he
also felt bad that he had to remind himself to
be patient with him.

Before the nurse's first visit, Bill had thought that the boy might heal and be left with just some scars. But he knew now that the boy's face was going to be very different, damaged for ever.

Bill offered the boy comics, but the boy looked at them as though he'd never seen a comic before and then dropped them with a total lack of interest. Maybe, Bill thought, it was hard to read with just one good eye. And so he tried to read a comic with one hand over his right eye. It wasn't nice, but it was better than not reading a comic at all.

The same thing happened when Bill showed the boy his toy soldiers, his collection of bomb fragments and the bird skull he'd found in Suffolk. The boy held each thing up to his face and studied it for a while. Then he put it down and never looked at it again.

It was all a lot harder work than Bill had imagined. He had thought he might be able to cheer the boy up, and despite his troubles they might be able to laugh and play.

Each night, Bill lay in bed thinking how all this felt like a test to see how grown up he was.

Chapter 11

Jane Snaps

Jane was scared of the boy. This was no surprise to Bill. Jane was scared of everything and the boy *was* unsettling. But Bill hadn't expected her to be so utterly terrified. He could see that she wanted to run away every time she saw him.

Bill thought that Jane was scared of the boy's hidden and damaged face. But when he confronted her, she said it wasn't that – she said she couldn't tell him what her fear was, that it was a secret.

"He's not what you think," was the closest she got to an explanation.

Bill saw how the bandaged boy continued to shadow Jane, gazing at her with that strange one-eyed gaze.

At first Bill was a little jealous at the thought that the boy was so obsessed with his sister, but then he became amused at her obvious fear. After a while even Jane's terror grew a little dull, and Bill tried to distract the boy away from her.

Part of the problem was their tiny house. Bill had never been one for staying indoors and his mother had been only too happy to have him out from under her feet.

But the boy could not go out. The nurse had forbidden it and Bill couldn't imagine how the boy could cope beyond the safety of their home. He knew that a crowd would gather to gawp after only a few seconds.

Bill had already caught some of his old gang looking in the window to try to catch a glimpse of the boy. Bill's house was taking over from the Dead House. No doubt the gang were telling creepy stories about the boy and daring themselves to get closer.

One day, Bill noticed that Jane was working herself up to say something. He could always tell. Sure enough, when they had finished their tea and the boy had walked away to sit on the sofa, Jane closed the door after him.

"Mummy," Jane said. "I don't think that boy should live here."

"Jane!" her mother said. "Don't be so unkind. He might hear."

"No he won't," she said. "He's got bandages round his ears."

"He can still hear."

"Not if we whisper," Jane insisted.

"Never mind that," her mother said. "Why would you say such a thing? Why are you being so mean?"

Jane tried to maintain her dignity, but her defences soon collapsed and she began to sob.

"He scares me, Mummy," she said.

Her mother put her arm around her and pulled her close.

"Shhh. Don't cry, my darling," she said. "It's all right. That poor boy has had such a terrible thing happen that –"

"It's not that," Jane said between sobs. "It's not just that anyway."

"What is it then, Jane?"

"It's him. The boy."

"We can't blame him for what's happened to him, can we, Jane?" her mother said. "It doesn't make him a bad person. You mustn't –"

"Not what's happened to him," Jane sobbed. "There's something not right about him. It's him that scares me, not what's happened to him."

Her mother loosened her grip and backed off a little with a frown.

"Now that doesn't seem very nice, does it?" she said. "He hasn't said a word, so I don't see how you can know anything about him. Has he done anything to you?"

"Not exactly."

"Not exactly? What does that mean? Either he has or he hasn't."

Jane stopped crying and scowled into her lap.

"Don't you think that poor boy has suffered enough?" her mother asked. "Before all this happened he was just a normal happy boy like your brother."

Jane shook her head.

"No!"

"Jane – stop it!"

"I know you think it too," Jane said, and her eyes were wild now. "Don't pretend you don't because I've seen you."

"Enough!" her mother said. "Go to your room."

Jane didn't move.

"This minute!" her mother shouted.

Jane ran up the stairs, sobbing and slamming her door behind her. Bill looked at his mother and saw that Jane had been right. Yes. Bill could see it now. His mother was scared of the boy too.

Chapter 12

A Visit

That Monday morning there was a knock at the door and there stood D.S. Henson. Bill was surprised to realise how pleased he was to see him.

"This is a lovely surprise!" Bill's mother said. "Come in."

Bill could see the look of hope on his mother's face. They had traced the boy's family, that's what she was hoping. He knew because he was hoping the same thing. He'd been wrong to want the boy in their home. It had been a big mistake. Henson seemed to see the look in their faces.

"I'm sorry, I should say I'm only here on a social visit," he said. "But I ..."

"No, no – of course," Bill's mother said. "I just –"

"You thought there might be news," Henson said. "I don't have any I'm afraid. We've drawn a complete blank. I wonder if we'll ever know."

Bill's mother bit her lip and nodded.

"How is the lad?" Henson said. "Has he settled in?"

"It hasn't all been ..." Bill's mother said. "I'm sure you ..."

Then she started to cry.

Bill couldn't remember the last time he'd seen his mother cry. She wasn't the crying type. She never had been. Tears sprang to his own eyes as he watched her. It was clear Henson didn't know what to do and he simply placed his hand over hers. His mother pulled hers away and reached for a hankie.

"Oh pull yourself together, Mary!" she told herself.

She wiped her eyes and blew her nose and in an instant returned to her normal self – or something that looked more like it at any rate.

"I'm so sorry," she said. "What a spectacle."

"No, no," Henson said. "I think you're being a bit hard on yourself."

"Am I?" Bill's mother said. "I have a husband suffering goodness knows what in a

P.O.W. camp and that poor boy has no one in the world and has been so badly hurt. And I'm here feeling sorry for myself! It's pure silliness. We all have to do our bit, don't we, Bill?"

Bill nodded, but it was Henson who spoke.

"You've done more than your bit. No one would blame you if you –"

"None of that," Bill's mother said, sniffing again. "I won't hear any talk of defeat. We won't win the war like that, will we? If that poor boy can suffer without a fuss, I'm sure we can –"

Just at that moment the boy appeared at the door, his one eye raking the air like a lighthouse beam. Bill saw Henson shift and frown before he faked an uncomfortable smile.

"There you are!" he said. "I've come to see how you're getting on."

The boy stared with his blazing eye at Henson and even Henson's fake good cheer seemed to leave him in an instant.

"Is everything all right?" he asked. "Are you happy to stay here with Mrs Marshall?"

The boy nodded, his eye still fixed on Henson.

"Well then," Bill's mother said, with a wobble in her voice and a twitch in her lips. "There you are. That's an end to it."

The boy remained standing in the doorway and stared at the group until Henson got to his feet.

"I better be on my way," he said. "I just wanted to see how you all were."

Henson left the house without a backward glance and Bill doubted they would see him again in a hurry. They were stuck with the boy and everyone knew it.

Later that day, the nurse arrived to change the boy's bandages. When she'd finished, Bill hung around in the hall as she talked to his mother in the kitchen.

"How's he getting on – with his wounds, I mean?" Bill's mother asked.

The nurse dropped her voice. "Well," she said. "I've been meaning to say."

She paused, at a loss for words.

"The surgeon wants you to bring him in. Next week. Is that all right?"

"Of course," Bill's mother said. "But is there something the matter? Is he getting worse? I don't want to –"

"No," the nurse said. "He's not getting worse. He's ... That's just it. Something very strange is happening."

"What on earth do you mean?"

"It's his ear, Mrs Marshall."

"His ear?"

"It's growing back – I'm sure of it."

"Healing you mean?" Bill's mother said. "That's good, isn't –"

"No, not healing – actually growing back. It's like he's growing a new ear. And not just his ear. His eye's growing back too. The surgeon thinks I'm crazy. It's not possible, but ..."

The nurse's voice trailed away. She looked back towards the room where the boy was sitting and Bill had to duck out of sight.

"It's a miracle really," she said, with a forced, nervous lightness in her voice. "I only keep the bandages on because, to be honest, you'd find it worse to look at him now, than before ..."

Her voice trailed away again.

"But listen to me," she said, and she got to her feet. "You must have things to do and here I am, rabbiting on. I must be off. Would next Wednesday be all right to come in? The hospital will confirm with you."

Chapter 13

Another Air Raid

Bill had been trying to remember the night the boy was carried out of the burning Dead House, but every time he tried, it slipped back into a fog, like a dream. It had been so vivid on the night it happened, but now it was vague and dreamy. The more he tried to bring it into focus, the harder it became to see anything at all.

Then one night, a couple of days after
the nurse's visit and after weeks of calm, the
air-raid siren sounded. They all hurried to
the shelter, with the boy between Bill and his
mother, holding a hand of each. It was the only
time they left the house together.

They sat in the shelter for what turned out
to be a false alarm. All the neighbours sat as
far away from them as possible, and didn't even
try to pretend they weren't staring. And at last
Bill remembered the night they found the boy.

He remembered his wish.

Bill remembered how they'd stood in the
street after the all-clear and looked at the
bombed-out house. He remembered hearing
the boy's voice and now he realised it was not a
shout at all.

The boy had said "Bill" and Bill had heard it
in his head, like a voice on the radio. Like his

own quiet voice in his head. That was why no one else had heard it. There had been nothing to hear.

Bill heard that voice clearly now and replayed it again and again. Had the boy lost his voice since the night of the bombs or was he able to speak like that – by transmitting his voice into another person's mind? Or was it just Bill's mind? And why had the boy never spoken again?

Bill had the terrible, chill sense of having begun something over which he had no control. But what could he say or do? Who would believe him?

The boy had come to replace Jane!

This was Bill's fault and only his fault. He had wanted a new brother, but one he could play with and have adventures with – not this ... this, whatever he was. What was the good of a brother like that?

This boy was a cuckoo, invading their house under false pretences. Didn't cuckoos throw other chicks out of the nest to make space for themselves? Was that going to happen to Jane? Bill almost cried at the thought.

Was that what Bill's wish had been? That he wanted a brother 'instead' of a stupid sister – instead of Jane? Is that why Jane was so terrified? Did she know that this boy had come to take her place?

That was why the boy was always staring at Jane, standing near her, standing over her. He was biding his time before he attacked her. Bill knew he had to do something before it was too late.

Should he go and see Henson? But what would he say?

I think the boy we found is actually the evil brother I wished for and he's going to kill my sister and take her place.

Bill shook his head. It sounded so silly when he imagined saying it to Henson, and that made it seem like it really was nonsense after all. But Bill knew it wasn't.

Bill vowed never to let the boy out of his sight, and to try his best to show more interest in Jane. And so later the next day he allowed her to rope him into one of her dolls' tea parties. The bandaged boy sat on the sofa and watched them the whole time.

As Bill was wondering how much longer he could keep this up, his mother came in to say that she and Jane had to go to the shops to buy Jane some new shoes.

Jane begged and pleaded not to go, but her mother insisted. Before they left, Jane came into the sitting room and pulled Bill as far as she could away from the boy.

"You shouldn't be in the house with him," Jane whispered. "Not on your own. He's dangerous. Make him go outside where everyone can see you. He won't do anything when people are looking."

Bill was touched by Jane's concern and he felt a fresh pang of guilt that he'd ever tried to wish her away. How could he begin to tell her that he was safe with the boy? It was *Jane* who should never be left alone with him.

"I'll be fine, Jane, honest," he said. "Don't worry about me."

"Come on, slow coach!" their mother called. "Stop dawdling."

Jane paused, looked at Bill and then at the bandaged boy – and then she set off after her mother.

Bill went to the front door and waved goodbye as Jane looked back. When they had disappeared round the corner, Bill closed the door and went to look for the boy. He was standing in the sitting room staring out the window.

It was time for Bill to be brave – to deal with the mess he had made. "I know what you are," he said.

The boy didn't respond or turn round.

"Look – you can't fool me any longer," Bill went on. "I'm not going to stand by and let you do anything to Jane. Answer me!" he shouted. "I know you can hear and I know you can talk. I heard you that night – the night we found you. Remember?"

"Yes," the boy said.

His voice was low but the sound of it made Bill jump. He backed off, wide eyed.

"Ha! I knew it!" he cried. "What do you think they'll say when I tell them you can talk? My mother and Henson and the nurse?"

The boy turned to face him and his one uncovered eye twinkled like a glass marble in the gloom.

"Who'll tell them?" he asked in a flat voice that sounded almost bored.

"Me!" Bill shouted. "I will. Why wouldn't I? People don't like being made a fool of. They don't like being lied –"

The boy started to walk towards him. Bill fought the urge to run and stood his ground.

"D ... Don't think I won't hit you, just because you're bandaged up and all that. I don't want to, but I will. I will!"

The thought of hitting that damaged face made Bill feel sick, but he clenched his fists and got ready all the same.

The boy came to a halt.

"You say you know who I am," the boy said, and the bandage puckered over his mouth as he spoke. "But do you? Do you really know who I am?"

Bill ground his teeth together and gave a nod.

"Really?" the boy repeated.

"Yes!" Bill shouted. "I know who you are. I wished for you. I wished for a brother and you came. But I've changed my mind. I want you to go. Get lost. No one wants you here. Go back to where you came from."

"No," the boy said. "I'm afraid I can't do that, Bill."

The boy raised his hands and began to fiddle with the bandages at the back of his head. As Bill watched he began to unwrap them. Bill felt his heart gallop in his chest.

"You're right," the boy said as he worked at the bandages. "I did come in answer to a wish. But it wasn't yours."

Bill staggered back in horror. All his efforts to prepare himself for the shock of what lay beneath those bandages was no preparation at all for the sight that greeted him now.

As the final bandage tumbled to the floor, Bill saw ...

His own face, in front of him – his own smiling twin.

Chapter 14

Bill and the Boy Alone

Jane wasn't in the least bit interested in new shoes. She worried the whole time she and her mother were out. She felt that she was the only one in the house who saw things as they were. No one seemed to understand that the bandaged boy was planning something. She didn't know what – but whatever it was, it was coming soon. She was sure of it.

There was something evil about him. Jane knew it. Everyone wanted to feel sorry for him because of his terrible burns, but she looked past that. That eye – that one eye. There was not one speck of human feeling there.

But it was more than that. It was more than knowing that he was evil. Jane felt responsible. She *was* responsible. She found it hard to admit that even to herself, but she was convinced it was true. When they got back from the shops, however crazy it sounded, she was going to tell Bill everything.

If nothing else, Jane had come to realise that the arguments and fights she had and would have in the future with Bill didn't matter. She would always love him. Maybe it had taken this strange creature who had invaded their home for her to remember that. She would tell Bill that too.

It took for ever to buy the shoes, despite the fact there were hardly any shoes in the shops. Jane would have taken the first pair that fitted, but her mother insisted they shop around.

On and on and on they went, while her mother chatted to shop assistants about the war and the weather and goodness knows what. In the end they went back to buy the very first pair Jane had tried on, in the very first shop they had visited. It felt like an eternity before they arrived back at the house.

Jane ran inside as soon as her mother opened the door. She skidded to a halt in the door of the sitting room, staring at the tangled pile of bandages on the floor.

"Bill?" she yelled.

Then she saw him, sitting on the sofa, face in hands, sobbing. Their mother came in.

"What on earth ...?" she cried. "Where's ... Where's the boy?"

"He ran off," Bill said. He wiped his eyes.

"Ran off?" his mother said. "Where? What do you mean 'ran off'?"

"I don't know," Bill said, and at last he looked up at them. "We had this argument and he left. I didn't mean it. I tried to stop him but he pushed me away and ran off down the street. I chased after him but he was too fast."

"And he took these off before he went?" Bill and Jane's mother pointed at the bandages.

Bill nodded. He closed his eyes. A tear trickled down his cheek.

"Maybe that's why he ran off," Bill said. "Because I stared at his face. I didn't mean to stare. But it was ..."

He couldn't find the words.

"Oh, Bill ..." she said. "What on earth made him take them off?"

"I think he was trying to scare me. I told him to stop scaring Jane and he went all strange and then he pulled them off and I yelled at him. It's all my fault."

"You mustn't blame yourself, Bill," their mother said. "It's my fault for having him to stay with us. He was too damaged. Not just his body, I think. But we must contact Detective Sergeant Henson. He'll know what to do. We'll go to the station now and tell him so that they can find him and help him ..."

Jane and their mother still had their coats and hats on, and when Bill had put his on too, they set off to the police station.

"He won't come back, will he, Mummy?" Jane asked as they walked. "To our house."

Their mother stopped.

"No," she said with a stiff smile. "I think perhaps we've done our bit. Eh, Bill?"

Bill looked up with a weak smile.

"Yeah." He nodded. "I think maybe we have."

Chapter 15

Jane Tells All

Detective Sergeant Henson was very sympathetic. He said that he blamed himself because he'd led the Marshall family to take in a boy who was so damaged in his mind as well as his body. He said they mustn't blame themselves at all.

They gave a description of the boy to the police and fire brigade and the air raid wardens and the ambulance service, but there was no sign of him at all. Whoever he was, he seemed to have disappeared with as much mystery as he had first appeared.

The story made the newspapers the next day because of the interest there had been in the original hunt for the boy's family. But the new search turned up as little as the last. Everyone marvelled at how someone who looked so strange could just vanish into thin air.

One by one, neighbours who had avoided Bill's house while the bandaged boy had lived there now came round as if nothing had changed. They even felt welcome to gossip about who he might have been and where he might have gone.

Bill's mother was frosty towards these visitors at first, but it was not in her nature to hold a grudge. Besides, she was glad to have friends to talk to, neighbours to gossip with and to be part of the company of other adults again.

After a week or so, life had gone back to what passed for normal in wartime.

But then D.S. Henson had a hunch he couldn't explain. He drove to the Dead House and pulled off one of the wooden boards blocking the door. It was the first time he'd been back to the place where the boy had been found all those months ago.

Henson picked his way past the abandoned rooms and found him lying in the sitting room.

Moments later the policeman emerged from the house, holding the boy in his arms, wrapped in his coat. He had been dead for a few days. There was no mistaking the injuries on his face. It seemed he had gone there straight from Bill's house and sat there in the dark and cold until he died.

Bill, Jane and their mother, Henson and the nurse were the only ones at the boy's funeral. It took place on a cool damp day. Rain threatened but never fell, and a breeze trembled the tree tops above their heads.

Sad as it was, it felt like an ending and everyone there had a sense of something like relief. They would never have voiced it. They had done what they could, but now it was time for them all to move on.

The boy had been the link between them and when they shook hands outside the church, Bill's mother and Henson knew that this was goodbye. Henson would return to his police work, and Bill's mother would get back to waiting for her husband to return.

And so the family took on its old shape again. The sadness of their father's absence stung more than ever now they didn't have the boy to distract them, but they all felt that this was as it should be. They should miss their father. Life should be painful.

But Bill's mother was determined not to feel sorry for herself. Her priority must be to look after her children. She saw how Jane already seemed a lot brighter now the boy was gone, but Bill seemed quieter, more subdued than his old self. He seemed somehow changed by the experience. She thought how she would need to keep an eye on him.

One night, about a week after the funeral, Jane crept into Bill's room at night.

"I have something to tell you," she told him. "It's a confession."

"Oh?" Bill said. "It better be exciting."

Jane closed the door behind her. But at that moment her courage seemed to fail her and she struggled to say what was on her mind.

"I wished ... for a new brother," she said. She didn't make eye contact with him. "When we were evacuated to Aunty Kate and Aunty Emily's. I hated it so much and I hated you for loving it there. I hated you so much that I wished for a different brother who'd be my friend."

"I am your friend, silly," Bill said, with a smile in the dark.

"I know that now," she said, sniffing back a tear. "But I was angry with you back then."

"But not now?"

"Not now, no," she said.

"How come you didn't wish for a sister?" Bill said.

"I don't know," Jane said. "I should have – you're right."

"What's this got to do with anything anyhow?" said Bill.

Again, there was a long pause before Jane spoke again.

"Well," she said. "You'll think I'm silly, but I thought that boy – that bandaged boy – was the brother I'd wished for."

"You did?"

Jane came over and hugged him.

"I'm just glad my wish didn't come true."

The new Bill smiled and his eye twinkled in the gloom.

Our books are tested
for children and young people by
children and young people.

Thanks to everyone who consulted on
a manuscript for their time and effort in
helping us to make our books better
for our readers.